MANAGED MAYHEM

NIGHTSMITH NOVELTIES COZY MYSTERIES
BOOK 1

PATTI BENNING

SUMMER PRESCOTT BOOKS PUBLISHING

Copyright 2026 Summer Prescott Books

All Rights Reserved. No part of this publication nor any of the information herein may be quoted from, nor reproduced, in any form, including but not limited to: printing, scanning, photocopying, or any other printed, digital, or audio formats, without prior express written consent of the copyright holder.

**This book is a work of fiction. Any similarities to persons, living or dead, places of business, or situations past or present, is completely unintentional.

CHAPTER ONE

Bridget Rowan hated her nose. It was long, shaped like a hawk's beak, and was at best, the perfect accessory to a witch costume on Halloween. Her nose had single-handedly wrecked her life not once, but twice. Also, it was currently running, which only made her hate it more.

She blew her nose, then folded the sun visor back into place and stared out the windshield at the swirling snow caught in the cone of light from her headlights. She had been driving for three and a half hours, but these final few feet felt like the only ones that mattered. Two months ago, she had been planning her wedding. Now, she was on the other side of the state, having fled the familiar in Grand Rapids for a few months of peace and quiet in the tiny town of Mill Creek, Michigan.

Driving across the state in a snowstorm wasn't exactly a promising beginning to what was supposed to be a relaxing, working vacation, but she had made it, so she supposed it could be worse. Her hatchback was idling in her aunt's driveway. The house loomed to her left, dark inside and out. It was one of the only homes on the block without any Christmas lights. It was a week after Christmas so she expected that would change soon, but the decorations certainly did a lot to make the neighborhood feel more cheerful on a night like this.

It wasn't the dark house she was focused on, anyway. It was the two-car, detached garage ahead of her. The building was set back from the road and had a second level with a small apartment. It was her new home until Aunt Agnes returned from her trip to Europe.

She eased off the brakes and let her hatchback roll forward until she was a foot away from the right-side garage door, then put the vehicle into park. She was eager to get upstairs and settle in, but she was dreading the battle with the cold wind as she carried everything up.

"There's no point in putting off the inevitable,"

she muttered to herself. She spent a few moments longer warming her hands in front of the heat vents, then double-checked the email her aunt had sent her to make sure she remembered the code for the garage door before she jumped out of her hatchback, hunched her shoulders against the wind, and scurried up to the glowing keypad.

The code worked. She didn't wait for the door to finish rattling open to get back in her car. As soon as she had the clearance, she pulled into the garage and shut her engine off with a sense of relief. There had been a part of her that was still worried that this offer was too good to be true. She would be making the same hourly rate she had as a bank teller, and she didn't have to pay any rent, all just to manage her aunt's little novelty shop for the next few months.

With her car off, the cold began creeping in quickly, so she didn't waste any more time in getting out of the vehicle. The garage was cluttered but well-lit, and the other space was taken by some sort of old convertible. She would be tempted to ask her aunt if she could take it out for a spin, but it didn't look like the sort of car that should be driven in winter.

The garage door opener and key ring were sitting on the workbench at the back of the garage, right where the email said they would be. Bridget quickly put both items on her own key lanyard, then popped the back of her hatchback to start unloading.

She started with the biggest suitcase first and hauled it out of the garage. The stairs up to the apartment were on the outside, attached to the right-hand side of the garage, but she paused for a moment to wave when she saw someone standing in the open doorway of the house across the road.

The figure waved back, then retreated inside. She wondered if she ought to go around and introduce herself to the neighbors, or if that sort of thing only happened in small towns in the movies. Either way, it could wait until tomorrow. A gust of cold wind chased her up the stairs, her suitcase bumping up them behind her. Someone had swept and salted them, which was good, because she was sure they would have been covered in ice otherwise.

The landing at the top of the stairs didn't quite earn the label of balcony, but it was big enough to hold her and her suitcase while she fumbled with the two new keys. The first one stuck halfway in the lock; that must be for her aunt's house. The second key slid in smoothly. The deadbolt unlocked with a click, and she pushed the door open, getting her first view of her new home.

Her first impression of the apartment was the

space, which was ironic since in actuality the square footage wasn't large, but the vaulted ceiling and pale blue and white of the walls made it feel bigger than it was. The floor was a pale faux wood, and at the far end of the open main living area was a large picture window that she guessed looked out over her aunt's back yard. The front entrance opened into the living room, and the kitchen was at the far end, with a divider counter partially partitioning the space. The kitchen table had a great view in front of the picture window, and she could already see herself sipping tea there in the morning. Someone had put a vase with a fresh bouquet of red and yellow daylilies in the center of the table, a splash of warm color against the cool hues of the room.

To her left were two doors; a quick exploration told her that the first one was the bedroom with a window that looked out over the driveway, and the second was a small but nice bathroom. The apartment was fully furnished, which was good because there was no way she was hauling her own furniture all the way out there for just a few months before hauling it all the way back. Whoever had done the furnishings had either been going for a Nordic style or really liked to shop at a certain Swedish home furnishings store.

Either way, the effect was minimalist and clean. It felt comfortable and homey, but not like it was someone *else's* home, which was good. She would have felt like an intruder if the little apartment was full of her aunt's personal belongings. Instead, it felt like a rather nice short-term rental, which it essentially *was*, except she got to live there for free.

"Not bad," she murmured. "Not bad at all."

It took another three trips up from the garage to bring the rest of her things in. She had packed as much as she could fit into her hatchback, but it looked like nothing at all once her bags were gathered in the living room. Most of her belongings were in a storage unit three hours away, and she wasn't sure how to feel about that. On one hand, she was sure she would realize she had forgotten something essential and would have to waste a day making the drive back to get it. On the other hand, she felt oddly light not being burdened by so much stuff. There was something freeing about it.

Plus, it would help her keep the small apartment neat and tidy. She was glad her aunt seemed like an organized person. If her store was as tidy as this guest apartment, then it should be a cinch to settle into her new role.

She sent her aunt a text message to let her know

she had arrived safely, copy and pasted the same message to her parents, then began the slow process of unpacking. There was no front closet, so her winter coat was hanging on a coat tree next to the door, and her boots were drying on a mat beside it. The lack of closets seemed to be a theme in the apartment, but there were plenty of drawers, cupboards, and wardrobes to store her things in.

She was halfway through organizing her collection of tea in one of the kitchen cupboards when her phone rang. Expecting to see her mother's number, she was about to press the side button in order to silence it when she spotted her aunt's name on the screen instead. It was three in the morning in France right now, and she had assumed that the older woman was asleep.

Whatever it was must be important, so she answered the call with a chirpy, "Hey, Aunt Agnes. Is everything all right?"

"Everything's great!" The volume of her aunt's voice made Bridget pull the phone away from her ear long enough to lower the call volume. She could hear music in the background. It sounded like Aunt Agnes was out somewhere, not like she had just woken up. "Do you like the apartment?"

"I love it," Bridget said. "Thank you again for letting me stay here."

She glanced at the tea cupboard and the box of food she still had to finish unpacking, then decided to put the phone on speaker so she could keep working. She wanted to get everything unpacked so she could start her first day of work at the store without having that hanging over her, but she couldn't exactly blow off a call from the very aunt who had offered her this opportunity to escape for a few months.

"Thank you for agreeing to keep Nightsmith Novelties running while I'm gone. Gene's always been the responsible one. It isn't like him to disappear like this."

"Hopefully he's all right," Bridget said. Her aunt's missing manager was a mystery she had expected to be solved by now.

"I'm sure he's fine. Now, it'll just be you and Kaycee at the store until the fifteenth. Noah should be back from his trip by then, which should take some pressure off you. Gene made a lovely employee handbook last year that should tell you everything you want to know, and you can call me if you need any passwords that Kaycee doesn't know. It should be easy enough to figure out. A smart girl like you won't have any problems there."

"I'm looking forward to seeing it tomorrow," Bridget said.

That was the truth. She hadn't seen Aunt Agnes in almost ten years and had never seen the little novelty store her aunt was so proud of. All she knew about it was what she had picked up through a decade of emails, phone calls, and birthday cards, plus a quick internet search when her aunt first called her to ask if she could manage the store until she got back from France this summer.

"Oh, you're going to love it. Have you had a chance to check on the house yet?"

"Not yet," Bridget said. "I can do it before bed, though."

"Oh, there's no hurry, sweetie. Take your time, and feel free to do it tomorrow if you're tired. I just wanted to remind you that you're welcome to help yourself to anything you find in the kitchen, and any linens you need for the guesthouse. Feel free to use washer and dryer in the basement, and there's some extra stock for the store down there too, if you start running low before I'm back."

"Thanks, Aunt Agnes," Bridget said. "I'm sure I'll have questions after I get to the store tomorrow, but so far, everything is just perfect."

"I'm glad," her aunt said, her voice softening. "I

told Kaycee you'll be in after lunch, and I'll make sure I'm available in case you need anything. Have a good night, sweetie."

After the call ended, Bridget filled her kettle and set it on the stove to heat. By the time it was ready, she should be done with the kitchen, then it would just be a matter of unpacking her clothes, toiletries, and the handful of books she had brought with her.

Then, bed… and after that, the first day of her vacation from the mess her life had become.

CHAPTER TWO

Her first morning in the guesthouse was peaceful. She woke up without an alarm and drank her tea at the kitchen table, accompanied by the beautiful blossoms while she enjoyed the view into her aunt's snowy backyard. Her cold seemed to be getting better, and her heart felt lighter than it had in months. She took her time getting ready for the day and familiarizing herself with the apartment, then spent half an hour shoveling snow on the driveway so she could get her hatchback out and go grocery shopping before she went to work.

It was her first time in Mill Creek, and the little town snared her immediately. With Christmas decorations still up under a fresh snowfall, it looked like a quaint holiday paradise. The route to the grocery store didn't take her past her aunt's store, but she got a chance to see part of downtown, and she could already envision herself walking down the sidewalk in summer in a sundress and a straw hat. It was the sort of town that was kept picturesque on purpose. With Lake Huron twenty minutes away, it was enough of a tourist hotspot for its image to matter, and the result was a lot of nicely maintained brick, ornate street lamps, and the snow-covered lumps of what she suspected were flowerbeds lining the roads.

The grocery store was smaller than she was used to, but it had the essentials. There was a supermarket about half an hour away, but Bridget thought it would be nice to spend the next few months living more simply. If she could make do with what she found in town then she would.

The less she bought, the better, anyway. She was up to her neck in debt for a wedding that never happened, and she intended to put every spare penny toward paying it off.

She'd planned to check on her aunt's house after she unloaded the groceries, but the sight of her next-door neighbor shoveling his sidewalk reminded her that she needed to do the same. She hadn't done any sort of yard work in *years*, not since she moved out of her parents' house and into first, a dorm room, then her first apartment. Shoveling the driveway that morning had been an unexpected reminder that she hadn't been to the gym since the breakup.

The sidewalk was easier, but it still left her breathless and took longer than she had hoped. She had just enough time to wolf down a sandwich for lunch before she had to leave for her first day at the novelty store. Checking on her aunt's house would have to wait until that evening.

Nightsmith Novelties was on the main road through Mill Creek, right in the heart of downtown. Bridget followed her GPS's directions and parked along the curb across from the building. She was more nervous than she expected, mostly because she didn't know *what* to expect.

The place was set in the corner storefront of one of the big brick buildings downtown. An old-fashioned wooden sign hung over the door, with *Nightsmith Novelties* written in ornate script, two carved roses crossed underneath the name, and the silhouette of a crow or raven above it. The effect was gothic and a little mysterious, especially when contrasted against the deli to the store's left, and the flower shop to the right.

The flower shop, *Belvoir Blossoms,* looked almost

painfully cheery in comparison. It was a standalone building with its own parking lot and a small yard in the back with a greenhouse. An ornate iron arch between the parking lot and the greenhouse was covered in pine boughs and Christmas lights, and the walkway to the front entrance was lined with wind spinners in the shape of flowers, birds, and insects.

The deli, named *Mill Creek Meats & More!*, had a flashing neon open sign, and a line of customers inside. Nestled between the two, Nightsmith Novelties seemed dark and quiet. No neon sign there, just another carved wooden sign in the window that read *Open,* next to a display of old books, a blatantly wrong globe, and a pocket watch resting on a faded purple velvet pillow.

At least it looked like her first day wouldn't be too busy. Bridget checked the rearview mirror to make sure she wasn't about to walk in with smudged makeup. Her hair, shoulder-length and dark brown, was down, and she had put on just enough makeup to bring out the best colors in her eyes. They were hazel, but sometimes looked more green, brown, or even grey depending on what she was wearing and what the lighting was like. They were her favorite feature, and though they didn't quite make up for her nose, she was glad she had *something* she liked about herself.

She looked fine, and she knew that at this point, she was stalling, so she forced herself up and out of the car and into the cold. She would have to explore the town more later, but from what she could see as she crossed the street, there were a lot of cute little shops that she wanted to check out. She hoped there was a place that specialized in tea since the grocery store didn't have a great selection.

She paused outside Nightsmith Novelties and tried to peer in through the window, but it was dark inside. With no idea of what she was about to walk into, she grabbed the handle and pulled. A cowbell rang above the door, and she stepped into a dim, cluttered building that smelled like incense and coffee.

"Hello?"

The front counter was to her left. It was more of a booth, cut off from the rest of the store by a waist-high wooden gate. The chair behind the counter, an actual recliner that looked like it belonged in someone's living room, was empty, and it was so silent that she wondered if there was anyone there at all until she heard a door creak shut somewhere out of sight. A moment later, a young woman with blonde hair drawn back in a short ponytail stepped into view around one of the cluttered shelves.

"Can I help you?" she asked.

"Are you Kaycee? I'm Bridget Rowan…"

"Thank God. Here are the keys." She pulled a lanyard off her neck and handed it over. "I quit."

CHAPTER THREE

"What? Wait…"

Kaycee ignored her. She brushed past and hurried out the door, not looking back as it swung shut behind her. Bridget looked down at the lanyard of keys in her hand, then around at the cluttered, dark store, and hurried out the door after her.

"Kaycee, wait! I have no idea what I'm doing."

By some miracle, Kaycee paused a few steps away and turned back to her. "Join the club. There's a binder behind the counter that should tell you what you need to get started. I'm sorry, I just can't do this anymore."

"Can you stay for just a few more days while I figure things out?"

Kaycee shook her head. "Your aunt is insane, and

the police were already here twice this morning. I'm done, and you can tell Agnes I mean it this time. Good luck."

Bridget opened her mouth to ask Kaycee to wait again, but the younger woman was already jogging across the road. She watched her go with a feeling close to panic.

"What did the police want?" she asked no one in particular.

A cold gust of wind answered her, and she had no choice but to retreat inside, where she took her phone out of her purse and tried to call her aunt. No answer.

She left a message to let Aunt Agnes know what was going on, then she started to look around in earnest. The cubby behind the front desk was cozy but crowded. The entire back wall was shelves, which held everything from books to gift bags to crystal balls and jewelry. Between the armchair and a small window that looked out over the sidewalk was a small table with an espresso machine and a jumble of coffee making supplies. An ancient cash register sat on the front counter, next to a card reader that looked at least a decade outdated. The shelves under the front counter were a mess of loose papers, folders, office supplies, and wrapping paper.

Charms, beads, and pendants hung over the

counter, low enough that they might have brushed her head if she was an inch taller, and fairy lights lined the edges and corners of the cubby. A dying sage plant sat at the far end of the counter, next to a crystal ball.

It was a mess. A cozy mess, but a mess, nonetheless. Bridget set her purse down on the recliner but kept her phone with her and looped the lanyard around her neck before she went off to explore the rest of the store.

One thing was certain; whoever decorated the apartment above her aunt's garage was *not* the same person who had organized this store. Calling it organized at all would have been a stretch. There was a wall dedicated to locally made crafts, clothing, and non-perishables, but the jars of honey and jam were mixed in with the candles, and half the clothing didn't even have price tags. Bookshelves held books, but expensive antiques sat next to used mass-market paperbacks. A low glass counter in the back held watches, rings, bracelets, and knives. The central parts of the store were pure chaos; the novelty store appeared to sell everything from Mill Creek and Michigan themed tourist souvenirs to antique furniture to art and the occult. She suspected that the

"Novelties" part of Nightsmith Novelties just meant anything her aunt found interesting.

And she had thought the lack of prices on the clothing was bad. Other than the items in the glass case, she was hard pressed to find a single price tag anywhere else in the store. The pit in her stomach grew deeper and deeper, and when she finally went through the door at the back of the store, behind the glass display counter, it got even worse.

The door led to what looked like a combined break and storage room, or maybe a hoarder's paradise filled with a jumble of extra items to sell. There was a tiny bathroom off to the side with an out of order sign on the light switch and a stack of brown paper napkins instead of toilet paper.

Bridget left the back room and staggered back to the front desk, feeling dizzy. She checked her phone just in case she had somehow missed a return call from her aunt, but no luck.

What was she supposed to do? She liked to think she was a smart woman, but she couldn't be expected to run a store she had never seen before on her own, with no one to show her the ropes... especially not when only about thirty percent of the merchandise had price tags! Was she going to have to work all day every day until the other employee got back from his vacation? And what did the police want? Kaycee said they were there *twice* that morning alone.

"I can do this," she muttered, even though she suspected she was lying to herself. "There's a binder with instructions. It shouldn't be hard."

She crouched behind the front desk, perusing the shelves for said binder. It took her a few tries to find the right one. There were two thick binders labeled *Sales* and *Purchases* that she set to the side before she finally located the slim white binder labeled *Employee Handbook*.

Straightening up, she looked around the store surreptitiously, but no one had snuck in while she was busy, so she sat down in the recliner and began to read. Almost immediately, her despair retreated to something a little more manageable. The novelty store might not have been well-organized, but the handbook was. Each page of instructions was printed on crisp white paper. Each page and each step were numbered, and the handbook was even split into sections. She skimmed the part about operating the cash register and the card reader, she would probably want to leave the handbook in reach to reference those the first few times she handled a transaction, rather than try to memorize the instructions now.

She flipped to the section on pricing next. *Prices*

are set only for goods ordered in bulk (incense, candy, some candles, cards, etc.) and items received on consignment or through local suppliers. Prices for bulk items are wholesale +5–20%, according to chart below. Items received through consignment or local suppliers should be priced as agreed per our contract with the source. All other items should be priced according to current market value (estimate if needed). Discounts may be given at employee's discretion, within reason.

Scribbled in pen beneath it was a note that read, *Never ask Agnes about prices! Look them up yourself.*

She looked at the included price guide chart. It was complicated, but not as complicated as she feared. She was going to have to look things up a lot until she started to get used to it, but she could follow instructions.

Bridget flipped through the rest of the binder and skimmed over the other sections. There were instructions for everything from electricity usage—keep it minimal—to how to clock in and out, and where to submit your hours for payroll. Whoever had written the handbook was a godsend. She wasn't certain, but she thought her aunt had said Gene, the missing manager, was responsible for it. If he ever turned up, she owed him a thanks.

By the time she finished skimming through the handbook, she felt almost prepared. Setting it down front and center on the counter next to the register, she waited for her first customer.

And waited.

When she finally checked the time and saw that it had been forty-five minutes since she arrived, she began to get worried. Was this normal for the novelty store? How did it survive without any customers? Maybe it was just the weather, or the season. People probably didn't have much in the way of spare funds with Christmas just passed.

When someone finally opened the door and set the cowbell off ten minutes later, Bridget straightened from where she had been slouched at the front desk, scrolling on her phone, and smiled at the newcomer; a slender woman in her late fifties or early sixties with short white hair and a wool sweater that had flowers embroidered on the sleeves.

"Welcome to Nightsmith Novelties. Is there something I can help you find, or are you just here to browse?"

She had her fingers crossed that the customer didn't need help finding anything, because she wouldn't know where to start.

"Sorry, hon, I'm not a customer," the woman said.

She approached the counter, her hand extended. "I'm Janet, your neighbor. You must be Agnes's niece?"

"That's right. Bridget Rowan," she said, shaking Janet's hand. "My neighbor? Oh." She took in the flowers that were embroidered on the older woman's sleeves and the floral scent that clung to her. "You're from Belvoir Blooms?"

"I am," Janet said with a pleased smile. "I'm the owner. I saw Kaycee walk off a while ago, and I suspect she hasn't come back. I just wanted to pop over and see how you were getting on without her."

"I'm not sure yet. There's an employee handbook that seems like it will be helpful, but no customers have come in yet, so I haven't been able to put anything to the test. Do you have any idea why she would quit like that?"

Janet looked around until she spotted a wooden bar stool near one of the shelves and pulled it over so she could sit across from Bridget. "I'm guessing you'll have more questions, and I have time to chat for a bit. Don't worry too much about Kaycee; she'll be back in a couple days. A week at most, probably. She walks out every few months, but it never sticks. I doubt it was anything *you* did."

"I doubt it too, mostly because I only managed to say about two words to her before she handed the keys over and left. She mentioned something about the police?"

"Oh, don't worry about that either," Janet said. "Nightsmith is the closest thing we have to a pawn shop in Mill Creek. If the police are looking for stolen or missing items, this is one of the first places they check. And with Gene still missing, it wouldn't surprise me if they were here asking questions about that, too."

"What do I do if they come back? I don't know anything about stolen items, or Gene."

"There should be a purchase record…" Janet got up and pushed through the swinging gate to the cubby behind the front desk. The space was small enough that Bridget had to move over for her and found herself squished back against the recliner while Janet searched the shelves under the counter. After a second, she withdrew the two binders Bridget had found earlier. "Here you go. If they ask about missing items, all you have to do is check the purchase record for the correct time period. It took getting in trouble with the law a few times, but your aunt finally started following Gene's system."

She set the binders down with a pat, then went back around to the front of the counter. Bridget opened the binder of purchase records and found that it was much better organized than she had expected, with tabs for each month and a polaroid photo of each item taped to its description, along with a photo of the seller's ID.

More relief. Maybe she really could do this. "Thank you," she said, the words heartfelt. "How do you know all of this? Are you friends with my aunt?"

Janet let out a very indecorous snort of laughter. "What do the kids say? It's complicated. Your aunt is a complicated woman, but I help her out when I can, and she does the same for me. I have to say, when she told me her niece was coming to watch the store, I wasn't expecting someone as normal as you. That's not an insult, either."

"Thanks? Is she really…" She trailed off, not sure what to say. Was her aunt weird? Crazy? Gossiping with a stranger about a family member didn't feel right, so she changed the subject. "Is it usually this quiet in here?"

"In the winter? Most of the time." Janet checked her watch. "But that's going to change in about five minutes."

"What do you mean?"

"It's almost three on a Wednesday." The older woman winked at her. "That means the folks from the nursing home are going on a field trip, and you're their third stop. It's about to get busy in here."

She nodded out the window. Bridget followed her glance and saw a small bus with *Huron Care Home* printed on the side pulling up along the curb in front of the store. The brakes squealed loudly enough that she could hear them from inside, and a puff of black smoke left the tailpipe. The paint on the bus was faded, and the fenders were rusty, but when the door opened, the people who began to climb out looked happy.

And excited.

And they were all coming for Nightsmith Novelties.

"Oh," Bridget said weakly.

CHAPTER FOUR

There would be no gradual learning curve for her; she was being thrown right into the deep end. She counted fifteen people who got out of the bus, sixteen if she counted the young caregiver who hurried ahead of them to open the door. The cow bell rang as the first of her customers came in.

Bridget scrambled for the handbook, not sure whether she should keep it open to the instructions for the cash register, or the price chart in the sales section. Her panic must have been plain to see, because Janet spoke up.

"If you'd like, I can stay and help you through the rush. It shouldn't be too bad; they're browsers, mostly. You might get three or four purchases from this lot. They're chatty, though—fair warning."

"Are you sure?" Bridget asked. The novelty store was slowly filling with the sound of chatter, and the open door had let a gust of cold in. "Your flower shop…"

"I have employees for a reason," Janet said with a wink. "Budge over. I'll handle the register while you handle the small talk."

Why the florist knew how to run Aunt Agnes' store, Bridget didn't know, and at the moment, she didn't particularly care, either. She moved aside so the older woman could fit better behind the front counter with her and plastered a smile on her face just in time for the first elderly woman to greet her.

"Look, Doris," she called out to her friend. "A new face. And who are you, dear? Tell me, is Hope here today? I was so hoping to see her. She's an angel."

Bridget opened her mouth, wracking her mind for any hint as to who Hope was. Another employee? She thought her aunt only had the two. Janet jumped in smoothly.

"I just saw her at the flower shop, Sally. She's doing great, the cold doesn't seem to bother her one bit. Let me introduce you to Bridget; she's Agnes' niece, and she'll be taking over here for the foreseeable future…"

She still had no idea who Hope was, but she shot Janet a grateful look as the conversation moved back to ground she was familiar with. She was a fish out of water, but at least she didn't have to handle it alone.

Bridget spent the next half an hour talking about herself. Forget running the store and making sales; Janet was right, this was more of a social excursion than a shopping trip for the folks from Huron Care Home. They made exactly three sales; a romance novel with a shirtless man on the cover, sold to an older woman who was shameless about wanting some eye candy to brighten her days, a pair of locally made wool mittens to a man shopping for his wife, who was sick with a cold at the nursing home, and some incense sold to Doris, who pressed a finger to her lips and handed over three dollar bills as she looked over her shoulder to make sure the caretaker wasn't looking.

"We aren't supposed to have burnables at the home," she explained with a whisper. "But I'm eighty-four years old and if I want some darn incense, I'm going to have it."

Janet didn't actually handle the register. There was no hurry, so she walked Bridget through it, and came up with prices seemingly from memory, which was good, since the gloves were the only item that had a price tag on them.

By the time the group from the nursing home left, Bridget was sad to see them go. She had a lot more time to chat here than she did at the bank, and seeing so many friendly faces was nice.

"They do this every Wednesday?" she asked once it was just the two of them again.

"Yep, rain or shine." Janet glanced at her watch. "Marla is probably wondering where I am. Will you be okay here by yourself?"

"I think I'll survive," Bridget said. "Thank you so much for your help. Really, I owe you."

"Oh, just consider it a favor for your aunt," Janet said. "I'll leave you my phone number. Call if you have any problems—here, or at the house."

She scribbled her phone number on the back of an old receipt, and Bridget took it gratefully. Janet might be a stranger, but she was pretty sure she was also an angel. She was a lifeline if Bridget needed it, especially since her aunt still hadn't called back.

"Thank you," she said. "If you ever need anything..." She trailed off, not sure what she could offer.

"I'll hold you to that," Janet said. "Good luck."

Bridget watched the door bump the cowbell as

Janet walked through it, leaving her alone. The novelty shop didn't feel quite as intimidating as it had before. She just wished her aunt would call her back, because right now, it felt like she had been stranded on a deserted island, and she didn't know when rescue was coming.

Nightsmith Novelties closed at six on weekdays, which meant it was dark by the time she got out that evening. The workday had only been a few hours, but she was exhausted—way more than she should be after the amount of work she had done. After Janet and the folks from the nursing home left, only two more customers had come in, and they both knew what they wanted and were patient with her flipping through the handbook to make sure she rang them up correctly.

In her spare time, and she had lots of it, she checked the sales record, hoping to find that this was just a particularly dead week. But when she looked at the numbers, she couldn't believe this place was still running. The novelty store had a couple of good months in summer—tourist season, she guessed—but those didn't make up for the rest of the year.

She looked high and low for an expense record but couldn't find one. It didn't matter. Unless her aunt kept a second sales report hidden somewhere else, there was no way she would be paying Bridget's wages with what the novelty store brought in, let alone all her bills.

She had been expecting to forget about her worries while she was in Mill Creek, not pick up more of them. With her shoulders hunched against the cold, she locked the novelty store. Next door, someone came out of the deli, letting a gust of warm, delicious smelling air out behind them. Pocketing her keys, Bridget turned toward the warm glow like a bloodhound, her stomach rumbling. She had food at home from her grocery run, but she was stressed and hungry and the deli smelled enticing.

The man who had just come out paused to look over at her. He was wearing a knitted hat and a dress coat, so it was hard to see much of his features, but he had high cheekbones and a nice, straight nose—her hatred for her own meant it was one of the first things she noticed on other people—and was handsome enough that she forgot about food almost completely as he called out to her.

"Hey," he said in a voice that warmed her despite the cold. "I've been hoping to see you. Have you had a chance to look for those…ah." His eyes met hers. They were grey, at least in the warm light that spilled out of the deli's windows. "Sorry, I thought you were Ms. Nachtschmidt."

"I'm her niece," Bridget said. "I'm watching the store for her until the summer. What can I do for you?"

"My apologies. I can see the family resemblance." He gave her an embarrassed smile. "A friend of mine's mother recently passed. Before she did, she sold a set of wooden statues to your aunt. They're part of a larger collection, and my friend was hoping to purchase them back. He spoke to the other employee, Kaycee, but she wasn't able to help him and said no one would be able to until the owner is back."

"Well, I don't know anything about the statues, but your friend is welcome to come to the store and look for them tomorrow," she said. She thought about all the extra merchandise in the back room and the fact that her aunt supposedly had even more in her basement, and added, "If he had a picture of them, I can check for them in the items we haven't put out on the floor yet."

She would have to try to figure out what her aunt had paid for them, too, but she wanted to help. Not just because this stranger was handsome, but because she needed something solid that she could actually *do*.

He looked relieved. "Thank you, I'll let him know. It was nice meeting you."

She smiled back at him as he gave her a nod and watched him walk away until he got into his vehicle. She had no idea who he was, but she wanted to. She *definitely* wanted to.

Enjoying the butterflies that lingered even after he left, she went into the deli, where she perused the menu behind the counter. There were more options than she was expecting, and a lot of them looked delicious, but after all of these changed she wanted something familiar.

One to-go bag with a toasted chicken Caesar sub later, she got into her hatchback and started the engine. While it warmed up, she unwrapped her sandwich, then told her car to call her aunt. While the call rang, she pulled away from the curb and headed toward home.

CHAPTER FIVE

The first call rang through to voicemail before she reached the end of the block. Sighing, she hit redial and took a bite of her sandwich. It was amazing. The bread was warm and toasty, and they didn't skimp on the dressing.

She felt a drip and looked down with a groan. Caesar dressing on her sweater, great. The call rang through to voicemail again, and she put her sandwich down and hit the redial button again.

This time, it rang once then went to voicemail.

Bridget stared at the infotainment screen for as long as she dared before returning her eyes to the road. It had snowed again, and the neighborhood roads hadn't been plowed yet, so she had to focus on driving, but her irritation was beginning to turn into worry.

Why wasn't Aunt Agnes responding? She had promised to be available by phone, but Bridget hadn't heard from her once, not a single text.

Instead of trying to call her again, she tried her mom instead.

"Hey, sweetheart. How are you settling in?"

"It's going well," she said. The response was more automatic than true, but she forged ahead. "Have you heard from Aunt Agnes recently?"

"No, and you know we hardly speak. I thought she was in contact with you?"

"She was," Bridget said. "But I haven't heard from her today, and I have some questions about the store."

Her mother sighed. "Just a day? Sweetie, a day is nothing for your Aunt Agnes. You know how she is."

"I'm worried. She told me she would keep her phone on her in case I needed to ask her anything."

"Well, your aunt makes a lot of promises. She doesn't keep all of them. Do you think you can muddle through without her help for now?"

"Probably," Bridget said.

Something lodged in her chest, disappointment. It was a familiar feeling when it came to her aunt, but one she hadn't felt since she was a teenager. She thought it was her aunt who had changed, but maybe she had just learned to stop expecting anything from her.

"I'm sure she'll call soon," her mother said. "How's the apartment? Do you like it?"

"It's perfect," Bridget said as she turned onto her aunt's road. "I'll send you some pictures later tonight. I think you'd love it. Hold on, I've got to go, Mom. Someone's at the house."

"Love you, sweetie. I'll talk to you later."

Bridget said her goodbyes and ended the call just as she turned into the driveway. It *should* have been covered in a fresh layer of snow, but someone had shoveled it, along with the sidewalk in front of the house. There was no mystery as to who did it, because he was still shoveling the front porch.

She parked in front of the garage and got out, trying to remember how much cash she had in her wallet. Was she supposed to pay this guy? If so, it was another thing her aunt had neglected to mention.

The young man stopped his shoveling and raised one gloved hand in a wave as she approached. There was an old cargo van parked along the curb that she guessed belonged to him… or maybe to his parents, because he looked almost young enough to be her son.

"Hey, can I help you?" he asked when she stopped at the bottom of the steps.

"I'm Agnes Nachtschmidt's niece," she told him. "I'm going to be staying here until my aunt gets back. Thank you for doing this. How does she usually pay you?"

"She's all paid up until June," he said. "I'm Tyler. I do the mowing and stuff too. I'm trying to make an actual business out of it. If I give you a couple of business cards, can you hand them out to your friends?"

"I'm afraid I don't know many people in town, but sure. Leave them with me and I'll see what I can do."

He fumbled with his coat and handed over a handful of loose business cards, then glanced over his shoulder at the dark house. "You're really staying here?"

"Well, in the apartment above the garage," she told him. "Do you come out every time it snows?"

"Uh, usually, but I was a little late this morning. I figured since no one was here, it didn't matter. But now that I know you're living here, I'll make sure I get to you earlier."

"Thanks," she said. "I appreciate it."

He only had a little more work left to do, so she

let him get to it while she went up to the apartment. With the tea kettle heating up on the stove, she settled down at the kitchen table and ate her sandwich while she gazed at the bouquet of daylilies. She wondered if the flowers had come from Belvoir Blooms. For that matter, she wondered who had left the key out for her, and who had made sure the apartment was ready. Another thing to ask her aunt… if the woman ever bothered to call her back.

When she finished, she changed into her pajamas, then dabbed at the stain on her sweater before deciding to run a small load of laundry. She needed to check on her aunt's house anyway, and maybe while she was there, she would find something to explain… everything.

She gathered up everything she could find that needed to be washed, armored herself in her coat and boots, made sure she had her phone and the keys, then braved the cold as she scurried to the house. Her key let her in through the back door, which opened into a dated, cluttered kitchen. The fridge looked like it was made in the fifties, and the walls were cluttered with pictures and photos of her aunt's travels. Bridget set her laundry basket on the kitchen table while she walked around. She had the same nose her aunt did, but somehow it looked striking on the other woman.

Maybe it was her confidence, or the way she dressed like she was about to walk onto the stage of some Victorian era play.

She ran the water and looked through the fridge to make sure nothing was moldering in there, then glanced through the rest of the house. Everything seemed to be as it should be, though given that she had never been there before, she couldn't be certain. Even if she *had* been there before, she doubted she would notice if something was out of place; the house was a mess.

It was *clean*, other than a thin layer of dust, but it held a jumble of clutter, antiques and oddities. She spent a long time staring at what she was almost certain was a real shrunken head in a bird cage before she shut off the living room light and retreated to the kitchen. She was very glad she was staying in the guest apartment, and not her aunt's house.

She wanted to get the laundry started, so the basement was next. Supporting the laundry basket on one hip, she opened the basement door and stared down the rickety stairs into darkness. She flicked the switch hopefully, but nothing happened. It was colder down there; it almost felt like a breeze was coming up the stairs and trying to push her away.

"I hate Michigan basements," she said with a sigh.

She slipped her phone out of her pocket and turned on the flashlight, then made her way down the creaking stairs. They were narrow enough that she had to move the laundry basket in front of her, so even with the light, she was walking down the stairs blindly.

Something crunched underfoot when she reached the bottom. Shining her light down, she saw sparkles of broken glass. Shining it up, she saw the jagged remnants of a bulb in the light fixture overhead.

Well, that explained why the light didn't work. Readjusting the laundry basket in front of her, she shone the light around the basement. Two thirds of it was dedicated to storage. A life-sized statue of the Virgin Mary nearly made her jump out of her skin, but she spotted the washer and dryer in the back left corner. They were newer units, bright red, and could hopefully run a small load quickly.

She took a step forward, then stopped again when a gust of wind blew a swirl of snow in front of her—two things that shouldn't happen in a basement. It only took her a second to find the broken window with her light. It was at the back of the house, and the pile of snow on the antique cabinet underneath it told her it had been broken for a while.

"Darn it," she muttered. This was another thing

she needed to talk to her aunt about, if she could get in touch with her.

Laundry first, she decided, then she would try to find a tarp or something to put over the window while the machine was running. She turned back toward the shiny red washer and dryer in the corner and took another step. This time, her foot landed on something soft.

"What…" She moved the laundry basket to the side and aimed her flashlight down.

A thin, balding man stared sightlessly up at her through cloudy eyes and a broken pair of wire-rimmed glasses.

CHAPTER SIX

"No, no, no, no, no."

Bridget ran up the stairs, her laundry basket dropped and forgotten. At the top, she slammed the basement door behind her, then turned around to stare at it, dragging in ragged gasps of panicked breath.

She didn't know what she was waiting for, but nothing happened. The house was quiet around her. The basement door seemed to stare back at her, still and innocuous.

Her hand reached for the doorknob almost of its own accord. She hesitated, then pulled it open just a crack, so she could aim her light down the stairs. Other than a few articles of her dirty laundry sprawled across the basement floor, nothing. The body was out of sight, hidden in the shadows.

Or... maybe she had imagined it? Not completely, she was sure *something* was down there, but her aunt had a lot of crazy stuff in her house. It could have been a mannequin or a wax figure. She was getting ahead of herself, and she would be mortified if she called the police and it was some sort of life-sized figure, not a real body.

She opened the door a little further and slipped through to the top step, then paused and glanced back, filled with an irrational fear that the door would somehow get shut and lock her down there with a dead body and no way out.

Well, there was the broken window, but it would still be a messy situation. She retreated into the kitchen and used one of the chairs from the kitchen table to prop the door open, then descended into the basement.

Her phone's flashlight was weak enough that she got halfway down the stairs before she saw the... body. She gulped. It certainly looked real, but then again, she hadn't seen a dead body since her grandmother's funeral five years ago, so what did she know?

She forced herself to keep moving down the stairs. There was something dark dried on the concrete next to the figure. It could be blood, or it could be anything else. She inched forward, careful not to step on any of the spots on the ground. The… splatter.

She crouched a foot away from him and a sound she had never heard herself make before forced itself from the back of her throat; something between a groan and a whine like a dying dog. This second look convinced her that she had been right the first time. This was no wax figure or mannequin. There was a dead man in her aunt's basement. This close, she could see a spatter of dried blood on his shirt, but it was really the wound on the back of his head that cinched it for her. Someone must have bashed him with something heavy.

There was something lying in the largest puddle of dried blood. She focused on it with her light; it was a small, wooden… arm? An actual arm, complete with a carved sleeve and tiny wooden fingers.

She had no idea what sort of murder weapon might have an arm. All she knew was that there was a dead man in her aunt's basement, and she very much wanted to not be there with him.

She didn't flee up the stairs this time, but she walked up them very quickly, pausing halfway to shine her phone's light around the room. She couldn't see much, not with her phone's dim light, and if someone was hiding behind all the junk in her aunt's basement, she would never know.

With a shiver that had nothing to do with the cold, Bridget hurried the rest of the way up the stairs and shut the door behind her, propping the chair under the knob for good measure. Pacing over to the side window, she looked out at the driveway as she dialed 911. It was a quiet night, made cozy by all the Christmas decorations that were still up, and it felt somehow wrong, given what she had just seen.

She had never had to call 911 before, and she stammered her way through explaining what was going on. To make matters worse, she didn't have her aunt's address memorized, so she had to ask the woman to wait while she checked her GPS history.

After that came the long, stressful minutes between when she called and when the police actually arrived. The red and blue lights lit up the street, and with a twist of her stomach, she realized this was going to be what all of her new neighbors remembered her for; she was going to be a woman who found a body in her basement.

She stepped outside to greet them, or rather, her. The woman who showed up looked younger than Bridget was, which threw her off balance, since for some reason she had always envisioned the police as gruff, middle-aged men.

"Are you the one who called about a body?" the woman asked. "Mind if I see some ID? Do you live here?"

"I don't have my ID on me," Bridget said. "It's in my purse, up in the apartment above the garage. I'm Bridget Rowan, Agnes Nachtschmidt's niece. She's the owner of the house. I'm staying here to take care of her store and watch her house while she's out of the country."

"Ah, I can see the family resemblance," the woman said. "I'll need that ID, but it can wait a minute." She held out her hand. "I'm Deputy Mariah Calhoun. Mind if I come in?"

"No, I very much want you to come in," Bridget said, stepping back. "Make yourself at home."

"In the basement?" Deputy Calhoun asked as she entered the house. Bridget nodded, and the other woman loosened her pistol in its holster and took a small but powerful flashlight off her utility belt. "You stay up here. I'm going to take a look around."

Bridget was very happy to wait in the kitchen while the deputy went down the stairs. She was gone for about ten minutes, and Bridget was just beginning to worry when she heard the sound of someone climbing the steps. The deputy shut her flashlight off as she reached the top. At some point, she had placed blue gloves on her hands, and she peeled them off slowly as she spoke.

"Right," she said. "I'm going to have to call in some backup. In the meantime, why don't you run and get that ID? I'll have some questions for you when you come back down."

Bridget went upstairs to fetch her wallet. It felt like a long time ago that she had eaten her sandwich at the little kitchen table by the window. When she went back down, there was someone else standing in the driveway, speaking to the deputy. Not another police officer—Bridget blinked at Janet in surprise before forcing her feet to move.

"Hi?" she said, feeling even more off balance.

Janet must have either seen the expression on her face in the dark or heard it in her voice, because the older woman gave her a kind smile and reached out to squeeze her arm.

"I live right across the street from you, hon," she said. "I'm sorry, I thought you picked that up when I said I was your neighbor."

"Oh, I thought you just meant with the store," Bridget said. She glanced at the house across the street. "You're the one who watched me arrive last night, aren't you?"

"That's right. I waved, but you must not have seen it."

Bridget handed Deputy Calhoun her ID, and while the other woman took down her information, she turned back to Janet.

"Did she tell you what happened?"

Janet nodded. "I can't be certain without seeing him, but it sounds like you found Gene." She grimaced. "Not exactly how any of us *hoped* to find him."

"What was he doing down there?" she asked. "I mean, the window was broken. Do you think he broke in?"

Janet shook her head. "I doubt he's the one who broke the window. There would be no reason for him to. He had a key. He was originally the one who was supposed to check in on your aunt's house while she's gone."

"That means he must have been here when someone else broke in." Bridget wrinkled her nose. "Poor guy. He had terrible luck."

"That must be what happened," Janet said. "He went missing right after your aunt left, so I wasn't even sure if he ever checked on the house. I looked for him here, but I didn't go into the basement. I didn't think he'd have any reason to go down there."

"Right, here you go, miss," Deputy Calhoun said. "Here's your ID back. Now, you said this is your aunt's house, is that correct? Does she live here alone?"

"Yes, as far as I know," Bridget said as she slipped her ID back into her wallet.

"What's a good way to reach her? Do you know where she is currently?"

"She's in France somewhere," Bridget said. "And I can give you her phone number, but I've been calling her all day, and I haven't been able to get in touch with her."

"France," Detective Calhoun muttered. She typed something into her phone. "What's the time difference?"

"They're six hours ahead of us."

"Right, well, no sense in calling her tonight. I imagine she's asleep. I'll take that number, and I'll hope we have a little more luck contacting her in the morning. Does she have a secondary contact or another way to reach her? Do you know if she's married? Does she have any family in the area, besides yourself?"

"She's not married," Bridget said, then added, "as

far as I know," because with Aunt Agnes, she was never quite sure.

"She's not married," Janet said. "She divorced the last one three years ago. As far as family goes… if I'm remembering correctly, it's just her two older sisters and then, of course, her nieces and nephews. None of them live nearby."

"Right. I'm guessing there's no chance any of her siblings or friends are traveling with her? I'm trying to figure out whether there's someone else we can call who can put us in touch with her if she isn't available by phone."

"No, she's traveling alone," Janet said.

"Thanks," Deputy Calhoun said, clearly unhappy. "And you… how long have you been here?"

"I got here yesterday evening," Bridget said.

The deputy gave her a sympathetic look. "Well, this is quite the welcome for you, isn't it? You said you're staying above the garage, not in the house itself?"

"That's right," Bridget said. "Um… can I sleep there tonight, or should I try to find a motel?"

"It should be fine for you to stay," the deputy said. "If you don't mind me taking a quick peek up there while we're waiting for the sheriff to arrive. He might have some more questions for you, but once he's done, you should be able to go back to your evening. Although, I would appreciate it if you'd give the station a call if you hear from your aunt."

"I'll let someone know right away," Bridget said, though privately she was worried it might be a while. Aunt Agnes was a lot of things, but reliable wasn't one of them.

CHAPTER SEVEN

The sheriff was an aging man who asked her to repeat herself enough times that she was convinced he was more than a little deaf. Despite that, he was kind and didn't seem too concerned that she might have more to do with the murder than she was letting on, which wasn't even something Bridget had worried about until Deputy Calhoun began asking her how well she had known Gene.

Thankfully, she had plenty of proof that she hadn't been anywhere near Mill Creek until the night before. According to the sheriff, Gene had been dead for at least two weeks, though he admitted it could have been longer than that, considering how cold the weather had been.

Part of Bridget was glad that the question of her

being a suspect was removed almost immediately. It was one less thing to worry about. Another part of her was deeply disturbed at the thought of Gene's body lying undisturbed in her aunt's basement for weeks while the quiet neighborhood went about life as usual. She had slept here, for goodness' sake. Yes, in the apartment above the garage, but she had slept on the same property as a dead body, and she hadn't even known.

She didn't go to bed until after the police left, and when she woke in the morning, not much had changed, other than a strip of yellow crime scene tape across the door to her aunt's house. She wanted answers. The who and the why seemed important even if just to know whether she was in danger or not. She tried calling her aunt three times while she made breakfast, but she didn't answer. She left the apartment a few hours later filled to the brim with worry; for her aunt, for herself, and for Gene's family and friends and what they must be going through today.

Compared to stumbling across a dead body, figuring out the ropes at Nightsmith Novelties hardly seemed worth complaining about. Not having price tags on most of the merchandise was the most urgent issue, but she found a sticker gun while she was looking through the shelves under the front counter and decided to begin tagging more items. Maybe her aunt had a reason for not wanting price tags on everything, but her aunt wasn't there, and at the moment she wasn't feeling all that kindly toward her. Her aunt had left her stranded in the middle of the ocean without so much as a life vest. If she didn't want Bridget to put price tags on things, she could darn well answer her calls and tell her why.

Pricing everything in the shop was going to take days. She started with the easiest items: everything that was bought in bulk from suppliers. She made her own list of prices in a separate notebook so she could easily reference it when she needed to. She was almost done with the incense when the bell over the door rang, and she looked up to see her first two customers of the day come in. She retreated to the front desk and tucked the sticker gun away, then greeted them with a bright smile, hoping desperately that not everyone in town had heard about the body in her aunt's basement yet.

"Welcome to Nightsmith Novelties. How can I help you?"

"Hello. I'm Lachlan Miller," the man in front said, holding a hand out to her. "We met yesterday evening."

"Oh." Her eyes widened as she shook his hand.

This was him; the handsome man she'd spoken to outside the deli, just without the hat on. "It's great to see you again," she said. "I mean, I'm glad you stopped by. Is this your friend who's looking for the statues?"

"That's right," Lachlan said. He had gorgeous, wavy, golden-blonde hair that she wanted to run her fingers through, except that was definitely a very bad idea. He might not be a customer, but she still didn't want to go scaring him away. He turned to his friend, who was dark-haired but a little taller than Lachlan, and gestured him forward. "Andrew, this is Agnes's niece. She might be able to help you."

"I hope you can," Andrew said, with a polite nod in greeting. He had his phone out already and turned the screen toward her. "Lachlan said you needed pictures of the statues. These are what I have. I had to go through some old family photos and crop them, so they aren't the clearest."

Bridget took his phone and zoomed in on the grainy photos. The statues looked like they were from a nativity scene. There was the Mother Mary, three wise men, and a few other people she couldn't identify on sight. Her family had given up on going to church when she was about ten.

The statues were small, about a foot tall at most.

They were made out of a gorgeous, deep red wood. She zoomed in further, squinting at the wooden figures. They were intricately carved, with robes and little hands that looked very familiar.

"Have you seen them?" Andrew asked.

Bridget hesitated. "No," she said, handing the phone back to him. "Would you mind texting me those photos, though?"

She didn't want to tell him about the murder, not if they hadn't already heard about it. But the photos might be important if the police were trying to find the murder weapon.

"Here, you can put your number in," he said. He handed her his phone, and she typed her number. Lachlan watched, his eyes narrowing.

"Thanks," Andrew said as she handed his phone back. He tapped on the screen a few times, and her own phone chimed. "I have no idea what your aunt paid my mother for them, but I'm willing to match her price to get them back. They're valuable, but to me they're mostly sentimental. My mom had them my entire life. I don't know what she was thinking when she sold them, but I do know she was having some money problems toward the end. I'd really love to keep them and be able to hand them down to my own children one day."

"Of course," Bridget said. "Let me look through the purchase records. Do you know what month she sold them in?"

"August of last year."

Bridget flipped through the sales binder. While Andrew waited, Lachlan reached up to fiddle with one of the charms that hung overhead, then said, "So, are you moving to town?"

"Just for a few months," she said, not looking up as she ran her finger down the list of purchases in August. "My aunt's coming back this summer, and I'm not sure how much I'll be needed at the store after that."

"Is it just you up here?" he asked.

"Mm-hmm," she said, distracted.

"Your boyfriend didn't come with you?"

She looked up at him, and he looked back innocently. "I'm not seeing anyone at the moment." She looked down and jabbed her finger at the purchase binder. "Here it is. It looks like Agnes paid two-hundred dollars for a set of—" she squinted— "'medium-sized nativity statues, carved wood.'"

Andrew, who had been giving his friend a vaguely irritated look while he distracted her, made a disgusted noise. "That's a fraction of what they're worth."

"Well, let me check the sales records," Bridget said. "I should be able to tell you if we still have them."

He waited impatiently while she skimmed through the sales records up until the current day.

"Unless they were sold under some other description, I'm not seeing them," she said. "So that's the good news. The bad news is I have no idea where my aunt would have put them." She was also a little worried that one of them might have been used to bash a man to death, but she didn't say that. She couldn't exactly go and look in the basement right now, either. "I'll keep an eye out for them, but I'm still getting settled in, so it might take some time."

"I guess that's all I can ask for," he muttered. "Thanks for helping. Sorry if I seem irritated. I know none of this is your fault."

"Trust me, it's completely fine," Bridget said. "I'm more than a little irritated with my aunt right now, myself."

Andrew turned to go, but Lachlan didn't budge. "Have you had a chance to explore town yet?"

"Not yet," Bridget said. "I've been here less than forty-eight hours, and most of that has been working or sleeping."

"You're going to love it," he said with a warm

smile. "There's a lot of amazing hiking for when the weather warms up, and if you like shopping, almost every business on Main Street is either locally owned or part of a small family chain. The council works hard to keep major chains out of the area. You'll have to check out the old mill, too. It's what the town is known for."

"I appreciate the recommendations." She had been planning on using this as a working vacation, but finding a body in her aunt's basement had put a damper on that. Maybe she should force herself to do something fun and try to get back to her original plan. "What happens at the old mill?"

Lachlan grinned as if he had been waiting for that question. "It's the old lumber mill, which the town was originally built around. It hasn't run as a lumber mill for nearly a century. Now, it's a cider mill. There's also an orchard, a Christmas tree farm, a corn maze in the fall; something for every season. Plus, it has a lot of historical significance for the town. It's worth seeing."

Since she was the only one working at the store now, she wouldn't exactly have much time off, but her hours were shorter on the weekend.

"Maybe I'll go check it out Saturday or Sunday,"

she said. "Thanks, and I promise I'll call if I find those statues."

She nodded farewell at Andrew and Lachlan and watched them go. She wished she'd looked around the basement a little more while she was down there; she might have found the statues then. Even if one of them had been used as the murder weapon, the rest might still be there.

Statues and cider mills would have to wait, though. She needed to do something with this store to try to turn a profit. She had promised her aunt she would take care of both Nightsmith Novelties and the house, and she'd already had an issue with one of those tasks. She didn't want to fail the other.

CHAPTER EIGHT

Bridget was beginning to understand why the store didn't open until eleven. She didn't get her first customers until after noon; they were a couple about her own age who chatted to her cheerfully while she rang them up. Without asking a single question, Bridget learned they were from Utah and flew out to visit family, taking advantage of the good travel deals after the holiday.

They bought a locally made, vanilla scented candle. The label read Mill Creek Lumber and had an ink drawing of an old-fashioned water mill on it.

She rang them up, wished them well, and then immediately got her next customers; a pair of teens who looked young enough that they should be in school. They dropped their backpacks by the door, and she was confused until she noticed the *NO BACKPACKS* sign taped to the window.

They seemed to know where they were going, because they went straight to the back of the store and didn't return. After a few minutes, she followed them and saw them whispering to each other while they pointed at knives in the glass case.

"Can I help you?" she asked.

They jumped, and the taller one turned to give her a polite smile. "Yes, actually, we were wondering if we could buy one of these knives."

"Do you have ID?" she asked. She wasn't sure of the laws, but she suspected she shouldn't sell a knife to someone who was under eighteen.

They exchanged guilty looks. "We're both eighteen," the taller one said. "But we left our licenses at home. We have cash."

"Uh-huh," she said. "No ID, no knife."

They left the store with a grumble, and Bridget returned to sticking prices on items with a vengeance. Normally, she wouldn't be so annoyed by the teen, but with only one legitimate sale three hours into the day, she was full of anxiety. She had no idea how her aunt kept this place running. She had to be missing something.

When her stomach began to growl, she realized

she hadn't thought ahead to lunch. She wasn't usually so scatterbrained, but she thought finding a dead body ought to let her off the hook for a lot.

She was on the phone with the deli, putting in an order for a ham and swiss sandwich so she could run over and pick it up when it was ready, when the bell over the door rang again. It wasn't a customer—it was just Janet. She waved at Bridget, then mouthed, Everything okay?

Bridget nodded and listened as the man said that he'd try to give her a call when the sandwich was ready, but they were busy with the after-school rush, and he couldn't promise he would remember. She thanked him and ended the call with a sigh.

"Sorry about that," she said to Janet. "I was ordering food. How long does the deli usually take to prepare a to-go order? I don't want to leave the shop unattended for too long."

"Oh, I can go get it for you," Janet said.

"I don't want to inconvenience you."

"I'm happy to do it," Janet said. "I'll pick something up for myself, too. I was just coming over to check on you. How's everything going today?"

"Well, it hasn't been a busy day," Bridget said. "I guess that's good because it's given me a chance to familiarize myself with the store a little more, but it's making me worry. I don't understand how this place is still running without any business."

"You, me, and the entire town wonder that, hon," Janet said. "Your aunt keeps it going somehow. I'm going to head over to the deli and put my order in. I'll be back in about ten minutes with our sandwiches, all right? You just hang tight."

They had one more customer while Janet was gone; an older woman who purchased an antique wooden jewelry box. It took Bridget nearly ten minutes to figure out what she should price it at. She managed to find it in the purchases' binder thanks to a piece of tape with the purchase date on the bottom and saw that they had paid fifty dollars for it. She looked up similar boxes online, took a guess at an appropriate price, and managed to sell it for a hundred and fifty dollars.

The customer didn't blink at the price, which told Bridget she might have priced it too low instead of too high like she feared, but with a three-hundred percent markup, she decided to be happy with the sale.

Janet returned a few minutes later with two wrapped subs and an unexpected companion. A lean calico cat followed her through the door.

"Um, is she supposed to be in here?" Bridget asked. For all she knew, it was her aunt's store cat.

"Oh, this is Hope," Janet said.

The calico jumped onto the front counter as if she had been there a million times. Bridget held her hand out to her. The cat delicately sniffed her fingers before bumping her head against her hand.

"You could call her a shared cat," Janet continued. "She spends her days visiting the shops on Main Street. She knows who's friendly and who's not, and who has the best food. I think she's decided it's your turn to feed her today."

"I don't have any cat food," Bridget said.

"Your aunt has some in the back, somewhere. I'll go look for it. You eat."

Hope watched her as she unwrapped her sub and took a bite. Under the cat's hopeful green-eyed gaze, Bridget had no choice but to cave. She tore off a small piece of ham and dangled it in front of the cat's face. Hope sniffed it, then gently took it in her teeth before gulping it down.

"You're pretty cute," Bridget murmured.

She was a stray, but the cat looked healthy. Her eyes were bright and shiny, and she had a flea collar around her neck and a nice thick winter coat. It sounded like she had a lot of people looking out for her, or Bridget might have been tempted to take her home herself. She missed having a pet.

Janet returned with a small ceramic bowl and a can of expensive-looking cat food, which she opened and poured into the bowl before setting it on the counter next to the cat. The three of them ate together.

"How do you know your way around the store so well?" Bridget asked. "Not that I'm not grateful for the help, of course. I just figured with the flower shop, you'd be too busy to help my aunt very much."

"Well…" Janet hesitated. "I don't mean any offense when I say this, but Agnes hasn't historically been the most reliable person. There have been a few times when she's left the employees here high and dry, especially back when my granddaughter started working here. That was around the same time Agnes was going through her most recent divorce. I took to popping over whenever your aunt was out to make sure things were going okay. Somehow, that turned into your aunt calling me if she needed some extra help, and well, I'm sure you can imagine how it snowballed from there."

"I didn't know your granddaughter worked here," Bridget said. "Does she still, or did she quit?"

Janet gave her a wry smile. "You saw her quit two days ago. Kaycee's my granddaughter. She'll be back.

I think she was frustrated by having to run the store on her own for the past two weeks. I'll bet you anything she'll be here on Monday, begging for her job back, and if she isn't, I'll talk to her about it and see if she wouldn't be willing to give this place another chance now that it's under new management."

Bridget had no idea that Janet and Kaycee were related, but that, plus her living across the street from Aunt Agnes, went a long way toward explaining how Janet knew so much about her aunt's life.

"It didn't even occur to me that she was running this place on her own," Bridget admitted. "You said Gene went missing right after my aunt left, didn't you?"

Janet nodded. "And he was the manager, so he was supposed to be doing the bulk of the work while your aunt was gone. I do hope you'll give Kaycee another chance. I know she didn't make the best impression on you, but given the circumstances, I think most of us would be a little stressed."

"If she wants to come back, the job is hers," Bridget said. "I'll take any help I can get. Does she know about Gene yet?"

Janet sighed. "Yes, I spoke to her about it yesterday. She's shocked, as you can imagine. I think she's having a tough time processing it. They didn't like each other very much, but learning someone you knew passed away unexpectedly and in such violent circumstances, that would be hard on anyone."

"What was he like?" Bridget asked.

"I'm not sure how to describe him," Janet admitted. "In a lot of ways, he was the perfect counter to your aunt. He kept things organized. Well, he did the best he could. He's the reason you have those purchase and sales records and that lovely handbook. Kaycee would describe him as a real stick in the mud, but he had to be if he wanted to counteract the chaos your aunt brought with her everywhere she went."

"Is there anyone who would want to kill him?"

"Oh, I'm sure plenty of people felt that way in the moment, but no, I don't believe he had any real enemies. I know why you're asking, but I'm inclined to believe that Gene wasn't targeted on purpose. From everything you and the police told me last night, it sounds like he was just in the wrong place at the wrong time when someone broke in."

"Then who would want to break into my aunt's place?"

"Anyone who knew where she lived and needed some money," Janet said. "She has a lot of valuable items. Even a quick burglary could net someone hundreds or thousands of dollars, and with your aunt out of town, there would be no one to file a police report until those items were already sold off."

"Then who knew she was out of town?" Bridget asked.

Janet paused and her gaze sharpened. "Now, *that's* a good question. I did, of course. The employees knew; Gene himself, of course, Kaycee, and then Noah—but he's been out of town since before Gene went missing. A few of our other neighbors may have noticed she wasn't there, but other than that, unless she told extended family members, I can't think of anyone she would have mentioned her trip to."

"What about the guy who does the yard? Tyler?"

"That's a good point. Tyler would have known, too."

"She doesn't have any other friends around town?"

"Your aunt makes friends easily but loses them just as easily. If she told someone else where she was going, I wouldn't be able to tell you who it was."

It was a mystery, which sucked because Bridget hated mysteries. Worse, she knew the statistics, and she knew there was a chance this case would never get solved. If that happened, it was going to drive her crazy for the rest of her life.

CHAPTER NINE

Nightsmith Novelties made a grand total of three-hundred dollars profit that day, which wasn't as bad as it could have been. If the store could bring that much in every day during the winter season, then maybe the more lucrative summer season could make up for it. But, as she looked through the old receipts and the sales records, she saw a disappointing number of days where they struggled to make even half of that, and too many days where they didn't make anything at all.

It was snowing again by the time she got home. Tomorrow was Friday and her last full day before the weekend. She needed to double-check the hours, but if she was remembering correctly, the store was open for five hours on Saturday and only three hours on Sunday, which meant her workload over the weekend would be lighter. Maybe she would go visit the old mill after all. Doing something fun would be good for her, and it might make her feel a little less despair about this move.

She tried calling her aunt again while she made dinner, then chatted with her mother for a while before she grabbed a book and retreated to the bedroom for the night. She awoke in the morning to find another four inches of snow on the ground, and to the pleasant surprise of seeing Tyler already halfway through with shoveling.

Her aunt might have paid him for the next six months, but that didn't mean the kid didn't deserve a tip. Bridget got dressed quickly, fished a ten-dollar bill out of her wallet, and headed outside to thank him in person.

"Oh, thanks," he said when she handed it over to him. "Makes me glad I moved your house up higher in my schedule."

"You're saving me an aching back, and I appreciate it."

She turned to go back in, but he called out to her, "Hey, wait. Miss? Is it true that there was a dead guy in the basement?"

She turned back toward him with a sigh. The news was starting to spread.

"I don't think it's something I should gossip about," she said. "But yes, I did find a deceased man in my aunt's basement."

"So, was it like a mummy, or like an actual person?"

"I'm pretty sure mummies are actual people," she said. "But no, it was a local."

"How'd he get down there?" Tyler asked. "Your aunt's nice and all, don't get me wrong, but she's kind of weird. Did she… you know…" He trailed off and gave her a pointed look.

"Are you asking me if my aunt murdered him?" Bridget asked. "No, she didn't."

As soon as the words left her mouth, she had to wonder. According to Janet, Gene had vanished right after her aunt left the country. Did that mean he had been seen after her aunt left, or did he vanish at the *same time* her aunt left? Had Aunt Agnes killed someone, fled the country, and left her to pick up the pieces?

"Then, like, how did he get down there?" Tyler asked.

"I have no idea." Bridget didn't want to give away too much. She didn't know exactly what the police wanted to keep secret. "Tyler, I have a question for you, and I won't be mad if the answer is yes. Did you happen to tell anyone that my aunt was leaving town for a while?"

"No, I'm pretty careful about that," Tyler said. "My mom always said you're not supposed to tell anyone you're going on a vacation until after you get back, and I figured the same rule applies to my yard care clients."

She nodded, acknowledging the good advice. "Have you seen anyone suspicious hanging around here?"

"No, just Janet, but I think they're friends or something."

"Yeah, they are," Bridget said. "Thanks, Tyler. I appreciate you answering my questions."

"Yeah, no problem," he said. He hefted the shovel and gave her a grin. "I'd better get back to work."

She returned to her apartment, where she took a shower and went through her morning routine. By the time she was ready for the day, Tyler had finished shoveling her driveway and sidewalk and had moved on to another house… but he'd left his van parked along the curb in front of Aunt Agnes's house.

Bridget stared at it. She knew Tyler had to be a

prime suspect. He knew exactly how long her aunt was going to be out of town, and no one would think twice if they saw his van parked on the street. He clearly knew what her aunt did and it was possible he knew the layout of her house, if he'd ever gone in to use the restroom or help her aunt with something inside.

Even if he *was* the one who broke in and killed Gene, he probably hadn't kept anything incriminating in his van... right?

But the van was *right there*. Wasn't it worth a look? Bridget bit her lip, then put her boots back on and went outside and down the stairs. She tried not to look suspicious as she walked down the driveway to the road. There wasn't a single soul in sight, just her and the snow.

She stopped by the back of the van and stared at the doors. Just one peek. Maybe she would see a box full of whatever he had stolen from her aunt. Maybe she would see nothing. It would only take a few seconds, and she wouldn't touch anything...

A car turned onto the block, making her jump back guiltily. She turned and headed toward the mailbox instead, watching out of the corner of her eye as the vehicle pulled into a neighbor's driveway. They parked, then sat in the car on their phone, so she just got her aunt's mail and went back inside. A part of her was relieved she hadn't gotten a chance to open the van; she was no police detective. She had no right to go snooping through someone else's belongings, no matter how much she wanted to.

CHAPTER TEN

Friday was the first truly quiet day she had in Mill Creek. The novelty store finally had a steady stream of customers, and she managed to get through the store's open hours without messing anything up too terribly. Janet stopped in to say hi, but for once Bridget didn't need a rescue. She closed at six and went home for the evening, and nothing terrible happened. It was wonderful. It was everything Bridget had hoped her relocation to Mill Creek would be.

She woke early on Saturday morning feeling well rested and a little at odds as to what to do. She didn't have to be at the store until noon, and other than reading, there wasn't much to do in her little apartment above the garage. She could go shopping again and buy more groceries, maybe meal prep, but what she *wanted* to do was visit Mill Creek Lumber and see what this town was all about.

So that was what she did. She put on some jeans and a nice warm sweater, her warmest boots and winter coat, and headed out the door with a single goal; have fun.

According to her GPS, the old mill was a fifteen-minute drive away, and it was a very scenic fifteen minutes. The route took her out of town and along gorgeous, winding, tree-lined roads. She passed a few farms in the first couple of miles, but after that, it was all just nature until she saw a large wooden sign pointing her toward the mill.

She made the turn onto a well-tended gravel drive, at the end of which she found a big red barn that seemed to be a storefront. Behind it was the mill itself, the waterwheel turning slowly in the creek. Off to the side, behind a wooden fence, was a large farmhouse. When she got out of her car, the warm smell of cider and donuts wrapped around her. She followed her nose into the red barn, where she saw a handful of employees serving customers at a long, wooden counter.

She ordered a cup of hot apple cider and a cinnamon donut, which was still warm when she bit into it. She sat on one of the long benches at the indoor picnic tables to enjoy her order. She would bet anything this place was insanely busy during the holiday season. The size alone told her that they were prepared to accept many more customers than they were currently serving, and she was pretty sure Lachlan mentioned there was a tree farm on the property too, which would draw people in droves through the Christmas season. Whoever ran this business knew what they were doing. She wished her aunt would take some pointers from them.

"Oh good, you made it."

She turned at the familiar voice…Lachlan again. She felt a spike of worry. Was he stalking her? She had no idea why he'd want to do something like that, but she also had no idea how he managed to show up at the exact time and on the exact day she decided to visit the mill.

"I decided to do something fun with my weekend," she said, giving him a polite smile. "Thanks for the recommendation."

"What do you think?" he asked, sitting down across from her. "Do you like the place?"

"It seems lovely," she said. "I haven't had a chance to explore much. I followed my nose in here as soon as I parked."

"Well, I'm happy to be your tour guide if you don't mind dropping some donuts off at the house with me first."

"Oh, do you know the owners?"

He gave her a rueful smile. "It's a family business." He stood up. "Fair warning, Andrew's here helping me work on an old snowmobile I'm hoping to get working. He's definitely going to ask you about the statues, even though I keep telling him you probably haven't had time to look yet. The man's obsessed, what can I say?" He turned toward the counter, raised a hand and made a gesture that the waitress seemed to understand because she nodded and began bagging a selection of donuts. Lachlan turned back to her. "Will you let me show you around?"

If this was his family's mill, then that explained why he was here, which meant he definitely wasn't stalking her. He was just being friendly, and she could use friendly right about now.

"Sure," she said, standing up. "I'd love to."

After he got his donuts and she finished her own snack, they walked down a plowed footpath toward the house together. Smoke came out of the chimney, and white Christmas lights framed the windows, making the house look cozy and welcoming, but that wasn't their destination. He led her around to the back, where a pole barn sat with its door open. Inside she saw an old car up on blocks and next to it, a snowmobile with its engine disassembled. Andrew was hammering away on something, but looked up when Lachlan and Bridget walked in.

He looked surprised to see Bridget, and set his tools down, wiping his hands on his jeans as he stood up. "Any luck with the statues?"

"Not yet," she said. "I haven't had a chance to look."

That much was true, mostly. She had the time, but not the ability. If the statues were anywhere, they had to be in the basement; she was almost certain the broken wooden arm she found next to Gene's body belonged to one of them, and the police still hadn't said she could go back into her aunt's house.

"I'm going to give her a tour of the place. Why don't you come in, wash your hands, and have some donuts? It's about time we took a break from working on that old thing," Lachlan said.

"I think we've almost got it," Andrew said. "But the engine still doesn't sound quite right. Didn't your dad have one of those scope cameras somewhere? I want to take a look inside the pistons."

"Yeah, I'll look for it," Lachlan said. He passed

the bag of donuts to Bridget. "No sense in making our guest wait in the cold. You head in and wash up. And get some drinks out, while you're at it."

Andrew nodded and turned toward the house. Bridget fell in step alongside him. He led her through the back door and into a spacious, modern kitchen.

"You can sit down if you want," he said, nodding at the breakfast bar.

"Thanks."

She sat down and put the donuts on the counter in front of her, waiting in silence while Andrew washed his hands. When he was done, he turned toward the fridge and pulled it open.

"Can I get you anything? Beer, cider—the hard stuff—sparkling water? I think there's some soda in the basement fridge."

"The sparkling water is fine," she said. He handed her a can of something raspberry flavored and took a bottle of beer for himself. "Thanks."

"No problemo," he said. "You think you'll have a chance to look for those statues soon?"

"Hopefully," she said. "I'm sorry it's taking so long. You must be frustrated. I would be too, especially considering how little my aunt paid for them."

Andrew scoffed. "Everyone in town knows not to

sell anything to Agnes if you want a good deal out of it. My mom should have known better."

"She must have been desperate," Bridget said.

"I don't want to talk about my family. It's still too fresh. What about yours? Are you all as crazy as Agnes?"

"I don't think so," Bridget said. "I knew my aunt was a little odd, but I didn't know *how* odd. The rest of us are pretty normal."

"Except for that nose," he muttered. She blinked, wondering if she'd heard him correctly, but before she could say anything, the back door opened and Lachlan came in carrying a large, heavy cardboard box.

"Bro, you'll never guess what I found," he said, setting the box on the breakfast bar between Andrew and Bridget. "It's the statues you've been looking for. They were in the back of the pole barn. I guess she didn't sell them after all."

CHAPTER ELEVEN

Andrew tried to set his beer down but missed the edge of the breakfast counter and the bottle shattered on the floor. Lachlan jumped back with a startled oath, then began grabbing paper towels off the roll.

"A little help, man?" he said as he began to clean up the mess.

Bridget glanced at Andrew. His face was so pale it looked like fresh snow. He didn't make a move toward the box, so Bridget did.

She pulled it closer and opened the top. It was full of the dark wooden statues he'd shown her on his phone. She began to count them, then her eyes landed on the Joseph statue.

His arm was broken off at the elbow, and there was a dark stain on the base; blood.

Andrew lunged toward her so violently that he knocked the box off the counter, and knocked her off her stool. She didn't even had time to scream as it tipped over, just tried and failed to grab for the counter, then crashed to the floor. Lachlan hurried around the breakfast bar to help her up. He pulled her to her feet, then rounded on his friend.

"What the heck, man?"

Andrew didn't answer. He was scrambling, trying to put the statues back into the torn box.

"Are you all right? You're not hurt, are you? What happened?" Lachlan asked, turning towards her.

"I'm fine," she said, rubbing her hip, which had taken the brunt of the impact. "It's the box…the statues. One of them has blood on it."

"It… what?"

He looked utterly confused. He was still holding on to her arm from when he helped her up, and Bridget felt a moment of uncertainty. Andrew was his best friend. Would he side with her, a stranger, or would he side with Andrew and help his friend keep this secret?

She took a deep breath. She couldn't let this go. If she pretended nothing was wrong and left, that would give Andrew time to dispose of the incriminating statue. It was wood; it would be easy to burn it to ash. She took a deep breath.

"The Joseph statue is missing an arm, and it has blood on the base," she explained. "When I found the body in my aunt's basement, there was a broken wooden arm next to it, covered in blood, and... and his head had been bashed in by something heavy." She paused, then because he still looked confused, she added, "Like a wooden statue."

"Body?" Lachlan asked, finally letting go of her. "What are you talking about?"

They hadn't heard yet, she realized. At least, Lachlan hadn't. Andrew was trying and failing to stuff the statues back into the box, which just kept ripping more and more.

She took a deep breath. "Have you heard about Gene..." She paused. She actually didn't know his last name, so instead she said, "He used to work at the novelty store."

"Yeah, the missing guy," Lachlan said, his brow furrowed. "Wait, are you saying you found his body?"

She nodded. "He was in my aunt's basement. It looked like someone had broken in through one of the basement windows. He must have been there, checking on her house, and gone down to see what was going on. Then…" She trailed off and pointed down at the statues. The Joseph statue was front and center, laying on its side, its broken arm and bloody base obvious for all the world to see.

Lachlan *still* looked confused. "Right, but if the statues were here this whole time…"

"I'm telling you, they weren't," she said. "They couldn't have been, because that statue right there is the murder weapon."

He opened his mouth, then closed it again. She felt a surge of frustration—he didn't get it—then she forced herself to take a deep breath. This was his best friend. Of course he wasn't going to believe some random woman who accused him of being a murderer.

Andrew reached for the statue and Lachlan turned toward him. "Wait, man, just wait."

Andrew glanced up at him. "You don't believe her, do you?"

"Of course not," he said. "But I need you to do me a favor and explain why that statue has his blood on it. And where'd the arm go?"

He looked down at Andrew, his expression hopeful and patient at first before it slowly turned to worry, and then something darker when Andrew didn't answer.

"Andrew, tell me what happened," Lachlan said, his voice turning more serious. "What's going on here?"

"I never meant to hurt anyone," Andrew said. He rocked back on his heels, looking up at them. "You've got to believe me. You know I'm not that sort of person. I feel bad when I hit a possum in my truck. I'd never hurt someone on purpose, but I've been getting the runaround at the store for weeks, and when I heard Agnes was gone, I figured if no one was going to help me, I might as well help myself, you know? I wasn't going to steal anything. I just wanted the statues."

"Buddy, you're scaring me" Lachlan said. Andrew looked down at the floor, ashamed.

"I broke one of the basement windows," he admitted. "Figured that would be the cheapest thing for her to repair. And dude, they were right there, sitting on some little table, all set up like my mom used to arrange them." He scratched his head. "I didn't think it through all the way, to be honest. How the heck was I going to get all of those statues out of the house without breaking them or hurting myself? I was trying to clean broken glass off the window when I heard the basement door open. I hid. I swear, man, I hid, but somehow Gene saw me, and he was making noise about calling the cops, all sorts of stuff, and I just… I panicked. I never meant to kill him. I just wanted my mom's statues back. I swear, man, I didn't mean to. I hid the boxes here in case the police searched my place, but I wasn't trying to get you in trouble or anything, I swear. I hated lying to you, but I had to pretend I was still looking for them so no one would suspect anything."

"It's all right," Lachlan said. Bridget turned to look at him, feeling betrayed, even though that was ridiculous considering that Lachlan didn't owe her a thing, and he had probably known this man for his entire life. "I know you never meant to hurt anyone. It's been hard since your mom passed, hasn't it?"

Andrew nodded like he was holding on to a lifeline.

"It's going to be all right," Lachlan continued. "Look, why don't you head back out to the pole barn and see if you can find that old scope camera of my dad's. I need to talk to Bridget and see if we can work something out with her, okay?"

Andrew closed his eyes briefly, relief making his features go lax. "Thanks, man," he said when he opened them. He stood up and gripped Lachlan's arm. "You're my brother, really, and I'm not going to forget it."

Lachlan watched Andrew go, then turned back to Bridget, who took half a step back. She was furious but also more than a little worried for her own safety.

"You're really just going to let him get away with it?" she asked. There was a tremor in her voice that she hoped he didn't notice.

"No," Lachlan said with a heavy sigh. He pulled out one of the bar stools and sat down, rubbing his temples. "Of course not. But you heard what happened last time someone threatened to call the police on him, didn't you?" He gave Bridget a sad smile. "He killed someone. If I don't do anything about it now that I know, and it happens again, then that's on me. I'm going to call the police. No, I'll call the sheriff directly. I'm going to ask him to roll up without the sirens and lights. You don't have to stay for this. It might get ugly."

"Will you be safe?"

"I'll be fine," he said. "After I make the call, I'm going to go out there and tell him I'm paying you off, then I'm going to spend a final few minutes with my best friend before everything blows up."

"As long as you're sure you'll be safe with him, I think I'll go wait in the cider barn." She paused and squeezed his shoulder. "You're doing the right thing."

He didn't say anything, just watched her go. She

went straight back to the red barn and ordered another warm cider, sipping it halfheartedly until she heard the commotion outside and joined the other customers in trudging out to the parking lot to watch Andrew get taken away in handcuffs.

EPILOGUE

Janet was right. When Bridget got to Nightsmith Novelties Monday morning, Kaycee was waiting in front of the door and begged for her job back while Bridget unlocked it.

"Please," she said as they went inside. "I know I made a horrible first impression, but you have no idea what the last few weeks were like. Or maybe you do. You've been running this place on your own since I quit, haven't you? So, you'll understand when I say I just couldn't do it anymore. But I shouldn't have quit like that, and I *definitely* should have stuck around to show you the ropes. Is there anything I can do to work here again? *Please?*"

Bridget had meant it when she told Janet she would accept any help she could get, but she didn't want to seem too eager. She crossed her arms and leaned back against the front counter. "How do I know you aren't going to quit again the second things get tough?"

"Because I'm actually a pretty good worker," Kaycee said. "I ran this place by myself for two weeks, and I didn't quit then, even though I really, really wanted to. I waited until someone responsible came along." She hesitated. "I, uh, sort of figured you'd know what you were doing, but my grandma says you didn't know anything."

That was… a true, if harsh way to put it. And Kaycee *had* stuck around when Gene went missing, even though it meant working seven days a week. Bridget took a deep breath.

"All right," she said.

Kaycee's eyes widened. "Wait, you mean it? When can I start?"

"Right now," Bridget said. She turned toward the counter, grabbed a pen and looked for a notebook. "Let's figure out the schedule, then maybe you can tell me how in the world this place stays in business."

Printed in Dunstable, United Kingdom